I0692460

William Cox

His Royal Highness the Comte de Paris

Genealogy and Incidents in the Lives of the Orleanists

William Cox

His Royal Highness the Comte de Paris
Genealogy and Incidents in the Lives of the Orleanists

ISBN/EAN: 9783337162825

Printed in Europe, USA, Canada, Australia, Japan

Cover: Foto ©Raphael Reischuk / pixelio.de

More available books at **www.hansebooks.com**

Philippe Comte de Paris

H. R. H.

THE COMTE DE PARIS

GENEALOGY

OF THE

D'ORLÉANS FAMILY

STIRRING INCIDENTS.

WEIRD SKELETONS IN THE CLOSET.

BY

PROF. LYNX.

INTRODUCTION.

At the time when the Comte de Paris is about to pay us a visit, it is not uninteresting, even setting aside all considerations of a political nature, to sum up the genealogy of this descendant of the Bourbons, who would ascend the throne of France (admitting that the country called him) under the title of Philippe VII.

COMTE DE CHAMBORD'S DEATH MAKES COMTE DE PARIS DIRECT HEIR.

By the death of Henri Dieudonné, Duke of Bordeaux, Count of Chambord,* the male line of the oldest branch of the royal family of France, issue of Louis XIV., became extinct. The only legitimate descendants of this monarch in a direct line, are the Bourbons of Spain and Italy ; but as these princes renounced, about two hundred years ago, their French nationality, in order to become sovereigns of foreign countries, they are excluded from the royal lineage of France by their own acts and by the effect of the laws, as completely as by the solemn declarations of their ancestors, which have been appended to the treaty of Utrecht. The French law expressly excludes from the privileges of French

---

* Born the 29th of September, 1820. Died the 24th of August, 1883, [See the Chronological Table.]

nationality all persons who have acquired a foreign nationality, and the first condition required of the civil status of a French prince is that he be French. It is therefore evident that if any pretensions to the rank and condition of French princes were put forward in their favor by blind partisans of legitimacy, they would be illusory and without foundation.

The first in order as legal successors of the royal family of France are the descendants of Philippe of Orleans, son of Louis XIII., and brother of Louis XIV., and the first place in the Bourbon family passes by right, in France, to the Comte de Paris, the head of the branch of Orleans. This fact was perfectly recognized by the Count of Chambord when he received the Comte de Paris in 1873 as his successor.

II.

COUNT de PARIS' GREAT-GRANDFATHER PHILIPPE-ÉGALITÉ.

THE FIRST SKELETON IN THE CLOSET.

He Votes For Death!—His Own Death on the Guillotine.

It will suffice to retrace in broad lines the career of the great-grandson of the Regent,

LOUIS-PHILIPPE-JOSEPH, DUKE D'ORLÉANS,

born at St. Cloud, in April, 1747, better known by the name of Philippe-Égalité. Ever since the year 1771, we see him acting in opposition to the court and signing the "protestation of the princes" against the dissolution of parliaments. Then rebutted by Marie-Antoinette, who had for him an instinctive antipathy, he takes openly, in 1776, sides against the queen, whom he accuses of secretly favoring the intrigues directed against Louis XVI. Then comes, after a period of idleness and dissipation in England, the affair known as the *Collier de la Reine*, when he takes an active part in propagating scandalous suggestions which compromise Marie-Antoinette. In 1787

2a

he appears in the assembly of the notables,
and makes himself remarkable by the violence
of his opposition.   Made Grand Master of Free
Masonry, he acquires a degree of popularity
which procures his election to the États Généraux, and is applauded by the crowd assembled
to see the procession pass through the streets
the day previous to its opening.   He is one of
the first members of the nobility who join the
deputies of the districts, and contributes to
the transformation of the États Généraux into
a National Assembly ; finally we find him in
the front rank of every revolutionary manifestation, and he is henceforth considered by
the court as aspiring to the crown.   Incapable
of acting such a part, having neither sufficient
tact to pursue it without compromising himself, nor sufficient force of character to throw
off the mask, and fearing the consequences of
his acts, he retires to England, there to await
the turn of events.   He had a party, attached
to him by reason of his great fortune, and for
awhile his champions talked aloud of raising
him to the power; but his weakness and in-
capacity paralyzed their designs, and he limited
himself to playing a secondary role in the
clubs, amongst the Jacobins and the Cordeliers,
in the district sections, which he frequented as
a courtesan of popular favor, of whom he expected everything without being able to impose
a single wish.   At length he was elected to the

Convention, where he took his seat on the *Mountain* (radicals' side) and voted for the king's death, accompanying his vote with the following commentary : " Entirely devoted to " the accomplishment of my duty and convinced " that all those who have assailed or who shall " assail liberty are deserving of death, I vote " for death !"

This vote, far from aiding the views of Philippe-Égalité, was reproached him by all parties, and aroused among none more indignation than amongst the revolutionists themselves. He expiated it on the scaffold.

Brought before the revolutionary tribunal, as having aspired to ascend the throne and conspired with General Dumouriez, he was condemned to death. Then he requests that he may be immediately executed, and the same day his wish was carried out (6th Nov., 1793).

When he was marching to his death the Abbé Lambert approached him with a respectful countenance and full of feeling. " Égalité," said he, " I come here to offer you the sacra- " ments, or, at least, the consolations of a " minister of heaven. Do you wish to receive " them from a man who renders you justice " and who bears for you a sincere commisera- " tion ? If you do not desire my ministry as a " priest, can I render you as a man any ser- " vices for your wife and your family ?" " No," replied the duke ; " I thank you, but I

"do not wish any other eye than my own on
"my conscience, and I have no need of any
"one to help me to die as a good citizen." A
member of the tribunal having come to ask
him whether he had no revelation to make in
the interests of the Republic, "If I had known
"anything against the safety of the country,"
replied he, "I would not have waited until
"this hour to say it. Moreover, I do not bear
"any resentment against the tribunal, nor even
"against the patriots. It is not they who
"wish my death, it comes from a higher
"authority," and he remained silent. On the
6th of November, 1793, at three o'clock, they
came to take him to the scaffold. He marched
with head erect, a proud look, with a firm and
assured step, and never exhibited as much as
on this supreme day the nobility and the dignity of his rank. He had become prince
again through the sentiment of having to die
as a citizen. While passing near the Palais
Royal he regarded for a long time the windows
of that dwelling where he had fomented all
the germs of the Revolution, tasted all the
disorders of his youth and cultivated all the
attachments of the family. The inscription,
"National property," chiselled over the door
in lieu and place of his royal escutcheon, made
him understand that the Republic had divided
his fortune before his death, and that this
palace, with its gardens, would no longer offer

protection even to his children. That image
of the poverty and of the proscription of his
race hurt him more than the axe of the
executioner. He bowed his head. The aspect
of the crowd which covered the place of the
Revolution, and the roaring of the drums at
his approach made him lift his head lest some
one should ascribe his sadness to weakness.
In approaching the guillotine, as the priest
continued to press him more firmly to accept
the resources of his ministry, "How can I
"in the midst of this crowd and of this noise ?
"Is this the place of repentance or of cour-
"age ?" replied the prince. Having descended
from the wagon and mounted the scaffold, the
executioner's aides wished to take off his nar-
row and tight fitting boots. "No, no, he said
"to them with indifference, you will take
"them off more easily afterwards. Be quick!
"be quick!" He regarded without blanching
the glittering steel. He died with a security
which resembled a revelation of the future.
As a republican, this prince has been calumni-
ated by all parties ; by the royalists, because
he was one of the greatest fomentors of the
revolution ; by the republicans, because his
death was one of the most odious instances of
ingratitude of the Republic ; by the people, because he was a prince ; by the aristocrats, because he had made himself one of the people ;
by the factions, because he had refused to lend

his name to the alternating conspiracies against
the country ; by everybody, because he desired
to imitate that suspicious glory that is denom-
inated the "Heroism of Brutus." Perhaps he
dreamed a moment of the royal crown, voted
by acclamation, but he was not slow to com-
prehend that the revolution would crown no
one and that there would be dragged down
with the throne all pretenders and all surviv-
ors of royalty. He repented then. The misfortunes of Louis the XVI. touched him. In
good faith he desired to become reconciled to
the king and to sustain the constitution. The
king received him, but the insults of the cour-
tesans and the antipathies of Marie-Antoinette
repulsed him.

In January, 1792, he presented himself at
court to pay his respects to the king. The
table was laid, and all the courtiers were present in large numbers. He was scarcely per-
ceived when the most outrageous epithets were
heard.   "Take care of the dishes!"* they
cried on all sides as if they feared that poison

---

*In allusion to his great-grand father, the Regent, who was
accused by the court of Louis XIV. of having poisoned the
Dauphin, his son, his son's wife and grandson, the four
having died in the same year shortly after one another.
Although it might be supposed that the Regent had reasons for getting rid of those who stood between him and
the throne, and as he had a laboratory where he could secretly prepare his poisons, yet history did not adopt this
theory, which we must likewise consider calumnious. We
should like to be able to say the same respecting the inces-

might have been put into them. They knocked against him, trod on his feet, and compelled him to retire. When descending the staircase, they spat upon his head and clothes. He left, justly indignant and more irritated than ever, thinking that the king and the queen had prepared for him this humiliating scene. The king had had nothing to do with it, but on the other hand he did nothing to palliate it. The queen was secretly flattered by this outburst of her favorites and by the humiliation of her enemy.

He then espoused extreme opinions as a safeguard. He threw himself into them in desperation. He found only shadows and the injuries of the popular leaders who would not pardon his name. He died without addressing a reproach to that cause and as if the ingratitude of republics was the civic crown of their founders. Unhappily for his memory, he became a judge of Louis XVI., and in a trial, where nature should have rejected him by reason of the ties of blood, he voted for death.

---

tuous relations he was suspected of having with his own daughters. Michelet, the great historian, takes up this view which was adopted by all Europe. Such we think could hardly have been the case with Mlle. de Valois and the Abbess de Chelles, but it is only too probable as regards the Duchess de Berry, whose profligacy scandalized even the corrupt court of her father, the Regent.

(For further details, which are too repugnant to be given here, see the memoirs of Mme. de Caylus, Duke de St. Simon, etc.)

The people in striking him, punished him less
than posterity. His life, a disordered one at
the beginning, tragical in its endings, commenced as a scandal, was continued as a plot
and finished as an act of resignation. He re-
habilitated himself to a certain degree in the
eyes of the mob and in the eyes of history by
the firmness of his attitude before his judges,
and by the dignity of his resignation in the
face of death. But the party of legitimate
monarchy has never pardoned him ; his memory is odious among his peers, and his descendants have been the more branded with
the original stigma, seeing that the son was a
repetition of the father, and that the role of
Louis-Philippe viewed in connection with
what followed, has been justly compared—in
taking into account the difference of the re-
spective situations—to that which Philippe-
Égalité played in the first revolution.

III.

THE COMTE DE PARIS' GRANDFATHER.
LOUIS-PHILIPPE I.

SOLDIER, PROFESSOR, PHILOSOPHER, TRAVELLER
AND KING.

His Visit to America.—His Accession to the Throne.
His Children.

OTHER SKELETONS IN THE CLOSET.

Louis-Philippe, son of the preceding, was
born in Paris, at the Palais-Royal, the 6th of
October, 1773. His mother, Louis-Marie-Adé-
laïde de Bourbon, was herself descended,
through her father, the Duke de Penthièvre,
from the Count of Toulouse, legitimated son
of Louis XIV., and of Mme. de Montespan.

In 1785, when his father Philippe-Égalité,
became Duke of Orleans, the young prince,
according to family custom, received in his
turn the title of Duke of Chartres, and was ap-
pointed Colonel of the Dragoons. He was

then twelve years old. These ridiculous pro-
motions were, it is well known, customary
under the old régime. From the commencement of the revolution, Louis-Philippe, still a
young man, followed the example of his father,
giving in, with éclat, his adhesion to the new
ideas. This is the usual tactic adopted by the
collateral branches in order to obtain popularity.

He entered the National Guard, took for his
only title that of *Citizen of Paris*, and had
himself enrolled a member of the Society of
the Jacobins.

At the age of eighteen, he took part in the
victories of Jemmapes and Valmy; but in
1793 he was proscribed, quitted the French
army and retired to Mons, to the headquarters
of the Prince of Coburg.

But he did not wish at this time to fight in
the ranks of foreigners against France, and,
like many other French immigrants, he had
to live by his talents and acquirements. As a
humble professor in Switzerland, with a salary
of 1,400 francs, he knew how to be content
with these small resources, and found, in this
more than modest position, the happiness of
the philosopher.

HIS COMING TO AMERICA.

A little later he left this country and visited,
nearly always on foot, the regions of the north
of Europe. In 1796 he came to America in

order to secure the liberty of his mother and brothers, to whom the directoire refused all freedom except on condition of the eldest son's going far away. He settled down in Philadelphia, where his brothers, the Dukes of Montpensier and Beaujolais, joined him. During his stay here, as also at the time of his departure from Europe, he was greatly indebted to Governor Morris, United States Minister in France, who generously assisted him with his purse and his influence, and rendered him all the services in his power. After several long travels in the States of the Union, and when the government was overturned by Bonaparte, the young Duke of Orleans returned to England and took up his abode at the Castle of Twickenham.

In 1814 the fall of Napoleon terminated the exile of the family of Orleans. The Duke returned to France and allied himself with the Bourbons, whose first restoration had just taken place. Although creating him prince of the blood, and giving him a fortune of three hundred millions, Louis XVIII., nevertheless, treated him with a certain degree of distrust and coldness, rendered perfectly legitimate in view of the role played by the father and the son at the commencement of the French Revolution.

When the *Hundred Days* arrived the Duke of Orleans retired to England, and returned to

France in the year 1807. In the midst of the
bloody reactions of this epoch, he main-
tained a prudent reserve, but without being
able to overcome the prejudices of the Bourbon Louis XVIII., who saw in him a pos-
sible heir to the throne, by means of a revolution, and who would not consent to grant
him the title of Royal Highness, which he obtained later under Charles X. It seems that
the old king well knew his relative's character,
as is shown by the following incident.

IV.

BIRTH OF THE DUKE OF BORDEAUX.

SHAMEFUL INSINUATIONS.

The Duchess of Berry, daughter of François I., King of the Two Sicilies, and of Marie-Clémentine, Archduchess of Austria, married in 1816 her cousin the Duke of Berry, nephew of the unfortunate Louis XVI. and of Louis XVIII., and second son of the Count of Artois (since Charles X.). She charmed the French court and attached to herself the somewhat fickle heart of her husband. At the age of twenty-two years, Louvel's dagger made her a widow. It is said that in her romantic grief she cut off all her hair, of a splendid blonde which poets have celebrated, and of which the duke was passionately fond. For two months she bore in her bosom a last and tardy scion of the ancient race of Hugues Capet, and the 29th of September, 1820, the duchess gave birth to a posthumous child, who received the name of Henri-Charles-Ferdinand Marie-Dieu-donné,* Duke of Bordeaux.

* Literally : Given by God.

This child was saluted as a blessing, and never before had the country been thrown into such a state of excitement. He was the latest offspring and the only hope of the dynasty. All France was in ecstacy—all France, except the younger branch of the house of Bourbon, which lost the throne of France at the very moment when it was about to occupy it. It was to this family a mortification and an annoyance which it was unable to conceal. From this moment one would imagine that some occult power was at work to give credence to the impression that the pregnancy of the Duchess of Berry had been simulated, and that a borrowed baby had been presented to the nation as the legitimate heir of the throne. Caricatures, songs, pamphlets were disseminated in profusion in the towns, in the suburbs, in the villages, and the d'Orleans were supposed to be the authors of this injurious propagand. The legitimist writers were unanimous in denouncing and censuring this manœuvre. Mr. H. de Lourdoueir, in his book "La Révolution c'est l' Orléanisme," recalls the following saying, which is characteristic :

"One word from this prince (the Duke of "Orleans) betrays the envious passions which "proximity to the throne had kindled in him. "When the birth of the Duke of Bordeaux was announced to him, he cried : 'Are we "then never to be anything in this country ?'

" Nothing ! He called nothing the position of
" a prince of royal blood and the three hundred
" millions that Louis XVIII. had given him !
" * * * Therefore, to make of this noth-
" ing, something, he secretly renewed all his
" practices with his father's former complices,
" and he commenced this new phase of con-
" spiracy by *protesting* in the English papers
" against the birth of the legitimate heir to the
" throne, basing this protestation upon infam-
" ous calumnies ; and when the king sought
" to obtain from him a disavowal of this docu-
" ment published in his name, he contented
" himself with a verbal denial, shielding him-
" self behind his dignity in order to refuse a
" public disavowal."

The chronicles of the times are full of
piquant details of these scandals, held up to
the public gaze, not only in France but abroad.
Sensational articles were published in the
Morning Chronicle under the initials S. A. S.;
and about the same time the Duke of Orleans
adopted towards Marshal Suchet a course
which greatly incensed the whole royal family.
" Marshal," he said, "I know well your
" loyalty. You were a witness at the *accouche-*
" *ment* of Mme., the Duchess of Berry ; is she
" really the mother of a prince ? As really as
" Monseigneur is the father of the Duke of
" Chartres."

These facts have not only been disseminated

by the public voice, or in the gazettes and
pamphlets of the period.   They are related by
the most serious historians and given in detail
in the *Histoire de Dix ans* by Louis Blanc.

But grave as are these grievances of the
legitimists against the Orleanists, they are
nothing compared with the incidents of the
residence of the Duchess of Berry at the
Castle of Blaye, as we shall see hereafter.

V

LOUIS-PHILIPPE'S ACCESSION TO THE THRONE.

The morning after the revolution of July, 1830, Louis-Philippe, whom King Charles X. had nominated lieutenant-general of the kingdom, entered Paris with the firing of cannon and the pealing of bells, and declared by a proclamation that he accepted the functions to which the confidence of the people called him, that he adopted the tricolored emblem—that of the nation—and that "the chart would henceforth be a reality." The Chambers were opened August 3d ; no notice was taken of the act of abdication which King Charles X. had signed at Rambouillet in favor of his grandson, the Duke of Bordeaux. The crown was offered to the Duke of Orleans, August 7th, by a majority of 210 votes.

The Chamber of Peers came in the evening to acknowledge the new sovereign. While Charles X. with his family embarked at Cherbourg to go into exile.

b

VI.

THE SECOND SKELETON IN THE CLOSET.

THE LAST OF THE CONDÉS.

His Tragical Death.—Was He Murdered for His Millions?

The commencement of the new reign was saddened by a tragic event, the dramatic death of the Prince of Condé, who had married at the age of fifteen, the Princess of Bourbon, paternal aunt of Louis-Philippe. Last scion of an illustrious family, but equally a stranger to the anxieties and perils of politics, the last of the Condés seemed to wish to throw into the background this name, which, by the death of his only son, the Duke of Enghien,* was on the point of becoming extinct, after having shone with such brilliancy in the last centuries of the monarchy. Confined to his little court of St. Leu or Chantilly, he indulged in hunting—his sole ambition.

Deeply troubled in 1830 by the misfortunes

---

* Shot by Bonaparte's order in the trenches of Vincennes, in 1804.

of his family, he did not deem it opportune to follow them into exile, and recognized without difficulty his nephew, Louis-Philippe as king of France.

The feeble old man was then entirely under the influence of a woman, whose name has often resounded in the polemics of the papers and in the prætorium of the tribunals. She was an English woman, Sophia Dawes, née Clarke, whose previous life was said to have been equivocal, and whom the prince had married to a gentleman of his household, Captain Baron de Feuchères, a loyal soldier, whose deceived good faith served to cover for some time the scandal of their illegitimate love. Endowed with a great spirit of intrigue, intelligent and gracious, greedy, imperious, insinuating, the Baroness of Feuchères had by her ascendancy, obtained the testamentary gift of the domains of St. Leu and Boissy in 1824, and later on several donations amounting to more than a million. But haunted by a secret uneasiness, fearing that the death of the prince would expose her to the attacks of heirs spoiled by her, and to the law suits to which she would be liable by reason of her use of undue influence, she had for a long time sought to unite her interests with those of the family of Louis-Philippe, so as to procure for herself powerful patronage when needed.

The truth respecting the relations of this

woman with the Orleans' family, will probably
never be known exactly.   What is certain is,
that in 1827, the pious Duchess-Marie-Amélie
(since Queen of France), wrote her very gracious
letters, encouraged her in her endeavors to have
the Duke d'Aumale (son of Louis-Philippe),
adopted by the prince as his heir, and warmly
promised her her help in the name of a mother's
gratitude.   It is painful, without doubt, to see
so virtuous a woman associate her maternal
tenderness with such solicitations which, to
say the least, were equivocal ; but this is an
admitted fact.   On his side, the duke followed
this matter up with that passionate solicitude
which the d'Orleans have always brought to
bear upon their affairs of personal interest.
Solicited, harassed on all sides, after long hesi-
tation, being weary of the struggle, the Prince
of Condé, finished by yielding, but not
without cruel anxieties.   The idea of leav-
ing the heritage of the Condés, valued at
three hundred millions, to the family of a regi-
cide, seemed to him a forfeiture and an impiety.
He however, contented himself at the first with
promises.   The then Duke of Orleans had a will
made out by one of his lawyers, Mr. Dupin,
in favor of his son, the Duke d'Aumale, which
it was proposed to submit to the prince for his
signature.   He, notwithstanding the promises
which had been wrested from him, always
sought to evade this and even considered the

necessity of tearing himself away from the obsessions and despotism of the baroness, by flight. He was assailed by fears of all sorts even to forgetting himself and saying before others, "when once they have secured what they want, my days will run plenty of risks."

At length after a fresh and exceedingly violent scene, between himself and Mme. de Feuchères, he decided upon making out and signing a will by which he instituted the Duke d'Aumale his universal legatee, and assured to the baroness a legacy of about ten millions. (30th August, 1829.)

This decided action did not bring him tranquility, and he gave way more and more to his puerile fears of old age and to his melancholy. The revolution of July happening here upon, increased the torments and troubles of the unfortunate prince. He had again reviewed his projects of flight, and he definitely fixed his departure for the 31st of August, 1830. The preparations were made in secret, but it seems impossible that the baroness was not made acquainted with them. On the evening of the 26th of August the prince went tranquilly to bed as usual. No unwonted noise or movement was heard during the night. The next morning when his valet, Lecomte, went to knock at his master's door, he received no reply. The door was shut from the inside, it had to be forced open.

A frightful spectacle offered itself to the view of those present. The prince was hung, or rather, fastened to the window handle by means of two handkerchiefs rolled one in the other. The knees bent, the feet dragging on the carpet, so that in the last convulsions of life he had but to get on his feet to escape death. This circumstance set aside all hypothesis of suicide, and struck all those who witnessed it. Public opinion was deeply aroused by this tragic and mysterious event and on bringing together a series of characteristic circumstances many persons were led to give it out as their firm belief that the prince had not taken away his own life, that he could not have done so under such conditions, and that he had been the victim of an assassination. The Princes of Rohan, collateral heirs began a trial against Madame de Feuchères for having made use of undue influence, which however, they lost. This woman, it is needless to say, was lying under the most terrible suspicions, and yet she was none the less received at the court, to the great stupefaction of public opinion, which called for a public inquest. An enquiry was commenced in the month of September, but nothing was neglected to stifle the affair. One judge, Mr de la Huproie, showing himself resolved to find out the truth, was suddenly put on the retired list. The redoubtable problem was

never cleared up. It is well to remark that
suspicions dared even to attach themselves to
Louis-Philippe : *Is fecit cui prodest*—unjust
accusation, doubtless, but which the new king
would have nobly repelled by repudiating a
succession, tainted with such suspicions,
which however, he did not do. But also,
if the Baroness of Feuchères was guilty
of a crime, which has never been proved,
it must not be inferred that the Orleans' family
have in any manner whatever been mixed up
in such an abominable action. But the great
fault of the then government was that everything that was necessary for a loyal and
severe enquiry to be made was not done, so as
to have brought the light of day to shine upon
this mysterious drama.

VII.

WHERE APPEARS THE THIRD SKELETON

THE ARREST OF THE DUCHESS DE BERRY.

Her Shameful Treatment and Her Public Dishonor.

After the insurrection of 1832 the duchess directed her steps towards La Vendée, where a great royalist movement, they had told her, would signal her arrival. But the peasants did not arm for the descendant of Henry IV. Madame wandered from one retreat to another, taking everywhere her hopes and her obstinate energy, but she was compelled at length to take refuge at Nantes in the mysterious hiding place which her friends had prepared for her. She remained there five months, engaged in the most active correspondence. The police were almost despairing of finding her, when the secret of her retreat was sold to Mr. Thiers for 500,000 francs by a converted Jew (Simon Deutz), mixed up with the legitimist plots and who possessed the princess' confidence. The miserable fellow left at once

for Nantes, being both watched and aided by
the police, and obtained two interviews with
his confiding victim. As he came out from
the last one, the authorities, informed by him,
invest the house, but, after the most minute
perquisitions, find no one. The duchess and
her confidants had had time to hide themselves
in an obscure chamber which had been made
behind the movable fireplace, and of whose
existence Deutz was ignorant. They remained
there sixteen hours, but at length gave themselves up, being half suffocated by a fire
which the gendarmes had lighted for want of
a better occupation. Up to the present time
all her adventures had a certain color of
heroism which compensated for what there
was of extravagance in them. The misfortunes of the Duchess of Berry only really commenced, however, with her captivity in the
Castle of Blaye, where she was sent by the
government and placed under the surveillance
of General Bugeaud. The unfortunate princess was destined, as the denouement of her
adventurous odyssey, to drink to the bottom
the cup of shame and bitterness, and the
government of her relative, Louis-Philippe,
avenged itself upon her in such a manner that
its immorality has been most justly condemned. In the month of January they
learned that the captive was suffering, and
that the symptoms of her indisposition led to

the supposition that she was *enceinte*. Doc-
tors were sent, and soon there remained no
doubt on the subject. She herself, led to it
by her condition, at length yielded and declared that she had been secretly married in
Italy to Count Lucchesi-Palli. The government, uninfluenced by the painfulness of her
position, instead of keeping silent and sending
to Palermo this conquered and henceforth
powerless enemy, gave to her declaration the
publicity of the *Moniteur*, employed every
means to obtain a public confirmation of her
state, and went so far as to have witnesses at
her confinement, of which they drew up an
official report. Louis-Philippe had now no
political advantage to gain from his unfortunate relative, whom he sent, humiliated and
broken down, to Palermo.

This shameful act created enormous excitement in France, and even those who were
hostile to the fallen dynasty protested with
profound indignation against a revelation of
such a nature. The reputation of General
Bugeaud, who was a loyal soldier, and who
had accepted the ungrateful mission of being
this woman's jailer, to certify to her shame,
was tarnished by it for the remainder of his
life ; and this act, motived by reasons of state
policy, has never been condoned by history.
How much greater reason is there, then, for
the strong feelings of resentment of the legiti-

mists' partisans, who will, on this account,
bear an eternal rancour against the d'Orléans,
the descendants of King Louis-Philippe, to
their latest generation.

VIII.

LOUIS-PHILIPPE'S STAR PALING.

HIS EXILE—HIS DEATH.

In the beginning of the year 1848, Louis-Philippe's star was paling on the political horizon, sombre clouds gathered and presaged a storm, electoral and parliamentary reform were loudly called for, but the Chamber withstood them. The agitation increased, and at length the revolution of February broke out, the Republic was proclaimed, and the king was exiled with the princes, his sons.

Louis-Philippe had been a modest, peaceful, and even homely king. He was wanting in that grandeur which in royalty is imposing ; having brought even to the throne habits of economy and foresight, he had asked the Chambers for doweries for all his children. Monetary preoccupations have always been a salient feature of the character of the d'Orléans. In Louis-Philippe's case, cupidity had become a state of senile mania, a fixed idea. One of the chief preoccupations of his peaceful reign was the establishment of his children in life. He married one of his daughters to the King of Belgium, another one to Prince August, of Saxe-Coburg ; his son Joinville to the sister of the Emperor of Brazil, and although his son the Duke d'Aumale was afflicted with a fortune of more than three hundred millions, that did not prevent him from being uneasy as to their future. He wrote despondingly to his Minister Guizot, in 1846 : " We shall never " establish anything in France, and a day will " come when my children will *not even have* " *bread* to eat." ' *Auri sacra fames!* * * *'

Louis-Philippe died two years after the Revolution, in his retreat at Claremont (England), where Marie-Amélie surrounded him with the most devoted attention. She herself lived to an advanced age, having lost in 1851 her daughter, Louise Marie, Queen of the Belgians, two of her daughters-in-law and several of her grandsons. She passed away peacefully in the midst of her own, the 24th of March, 1866.

HIS CHILDREN.

Of his marriage with Marie-Amélie, Louis-Philippe had for issue eight children—the Duke of Orleans ; Louise, Queen of Belgium ; Marie, Princess of Wurtemburg ; the Duke of Nemours* ; Clémentine, married to the Duke

---

* GENERAL THE DUKE DE NEMOURS, born in 1814, was supposed rightly or wrongly, to be a partisan of the ideas

of Saxe Coburg ; the Prince of Joinville,† the
Duke d'Aumale,‡ and the Duke of Montpensier.§   His five sons were brought up at the

of the former régime, a prince of a cold and haughty dis-
position, which had caused him to be called the "*dude* of
the family," and he was far from being popular.

The 3rd of February, 1831, the Belgium Congress chose
him for king, but Louis-Philippe, who saw that the
European powers were hostile to this election, would not
give his son the authorization to ascend the throne of Belgium, and followed the same line of conduct in connection
with the throne of Greece.

The duke fought with his brothers in Algeria, and was in
command of several expeditions against the Emir, the
Kabyles and Oran.

The Duke de Nemours had two sons : Le Count d'Eu,
born in 1842, who married Dom Pedro's daughter and the
Duke d'Alençon, born in 1844, who was authorized in 1871,
to enter the French army as captain of artillery.

† The Prince of Joinville was a commander in the
navy and attained the post of Vice-Admiral. He distinguished himself in Mexico, then in Morocco, where he
took part in the naval attack on their posts, and also in
the taking of Mogador. It was the Prince of Joinville who
was chosen by the king to go to Saint Helena to bring
home the mortal remains of Napoleon.

‡ The Duke d' Aumale.—*His exploits as a general.* Of all
the sons of Louis-Philippe, he is the most distinguished.
A remarkable episode of the war of Algeria, which
lasted several years, was the taking of the "*Smala*" by
the Duke. This young prince had been placed in command of a French column which was to penetrate to the
interior of the desert where Abd-el-Kader, the Arab Emir
had encamped his family and his servants. The "*Smala*"
of Abd-el-Kader contained a numerous population, rich
treasures and a quantity of beasts of value. The Duke
d'Aumale did not hesitate to attack it although he had only
500 men with him. Giving the command to charge,
he rushes forward with his cavalry, and the troops fall like
a deluge in the midst of the frightened women and de-
fenceless Arabs. The confusion is inexpressible, the tents

College Henry IV., and received, consequently,
a public education.

are overturned ; the provisions, jewels, rich hangings and
accessories of all kinds, are scattered on all sides ; the
horses eat the dust, the flocks of sheep take flight; in vain the
sons of the desert endeavor to struggle with their impetuous
enemies ; nothing is able to withstand the French cavalry.
Masters of the position, our soldiers take more than 400
prisoners and carry off immense quantities of spoils (1843).
This day was decisive in its results ; a defeat was inflicted
upon the Emir which was the first step in the direction of
complete submission.   The exploit of the Duke d'Aumale
has been reproduced by the painter, Horace Vernet, in a
gigantic and splendid picture, which has been placed in
the museum of Versailles.   He presided at the Court which
sentenced to death the traitor Bazaine. The Duke is a distinguished man of letters ; his literary works have obtained
for him a seat in the French Academy, and his social charms
have made him an important personality in the Parisian
wor.d.   The government has allowed him to return and to
reside in France.

§ THE DUKE DE MONTPENSIER, youngest son of Louis-
Phillipe, born in 1824, served as his brothers in Algeria,
then visited the countries of the East, and married in
1846, the sister of the Queen of Spain, Isabella II. The
duke, become Infant of Spain, settled down in that
country after 1848, and had to take a part in all the crises
which agitated his adopted country.   In March, 1870, he
killed in a duel the Prince Henri de Bourbon, brother
of the ex-king of Spain, François d'Assise.

He had six children, two sons and four daughters, one
of whom married her first cousin, the Count de Paris.

IX.

THE COMTE DE PARIS' FATHER.

A GALLANT SOLDIER.

A Favorite of the People—His Tragic and Premature Death.

Ferdinand – Philippe –Louis–Charles – Henri, Duke of Chartres, eldest son of the King Louis-Philippe, was born at Palermo, the 3rd Sept., 1810. On his father's accession to the throne, his title of Duke of Chartres was exchanged for that of Duke d'Orléans, and prince of the royal blood.

Sent to Lyons in 1831, to re establish order, we find him endeavoring, by his extreme moderation, to calm the popular irritation and using his influence to prevent those who had been led into rebellion by hunger and want, from being treated with rigour. The cholera, which ravaged Paris in 1832, furnished him with a fresh opportunity for distinguishing himself. He visited the hospitals when the scourge was at its worst and received on this occasion a medal from the Municipal Council of Paris.

At the end of this same year, on the outbreak
of the war with Belgium, he commanded the
brigade of the Vanguard, assisted at the oper-
ations which led to the taking of Antwerp, and
fought bravely during the attack of St. Laurent.
In 1835, the Duke went to Africa, was wounded
at the battle of Habrah, fell seriously ill from
the effects of long sustained fatigues, and returned to France. In 1836, when traveling in
Germany, he met the Princess of Mecklenburg,
whom he married, in Paris, the 30th May, 1837.
On the occasion of the fetes given in honor of
the event, many persons were crushed to death
on the Champ de Mars. On hearing of these
misfortunes, Princess Helena cried out, "It is
the same as at the fetes of Louis XVI. What
a frightful omen!" During one of the sittings
of the Chamber of Peers, the Marquis of Dreux-
Brézé, having blamed the Duke for having
married a protestant, he replied in these remarkable words: "I see inscribed in our fun-
damental code, in the first line, religious liberty
as the most precious of all the liberties granted
to the French; I do not understand why the
Royal Family alone should be excluded from
this benefit, which is perfectly in harmony
with the reigning sentiments of French society."

In 1839 the Duke of Orleans returned to Algeria, assumed the command of a division, and
crossed the "portes de fer," hitherto deemed un-

passable. Next year, accompanied by his young brother, the Duke d'Aumale, he conducted his last and most brilliant campaign. The courage which he showed at the battles of Affroum, l'Oued Ger, the Bois des Oliviers, at the taking of Medeah, and especially at that of Tenia de Mauzaia, when he commanded in person the attacking column, do him the greatest honor.

Shortly afterwards he bade adieu to the army of Africa and returned to Paris, where he organized the Chasseurs a Pied de Vincennes. He was returning from the waters of Plombières, where he had taken his wife, and was arranging to join the camp cf St Omer, when, going to Neuilly to bid good-bye to his family, the horses of his carriage darted off in front of the Porte-Maillot. Was it that he wished to jump out, or that he was thrown out by a shock, he fell head foremost on the pavement, and ruptured the vertebral column. Borne to a neighboring house, he expired a few moments after, the 13th July, 1842. After having been exposed five days in Notre-Dame, his body was transported to the family vault at Dreux.

He possessed every quality necessary to seduce the masses and would probably have made a popular king, and have saved the d'Orléans monarchy in 1848, had not this tragic event carried him off so unfortunately.

Of his marriage with Princess Helena he had two sons,

LOUIS-PHILIPPE, ALBERT D'ORLÉANS,

COMTE DE PARIS,

born in Paris the 24th of August, 1838, and

ROBERT-PHILIPPE-LOUIS-EUGÈNE FERDINAND,

DUKE OF CHARTRES,[*]

born in Paris, in 1840.

---

[*] The Duke of Chartres married—June 11th, 1863, at Kingston, on Thames,—Françoise, the daughter of his uncle, the Prince of Joinville, following in this the example set by his brother, the Comte de Paris. It is evident that these inter-marriages were entered into with the object of retaining in the family their immense fortunes.

Of their marriage they had issue :

Marie-Amélie Françoise-Hélène, born in 1865 and married in 1885 to Waldemar, Prince of Denmark.

Henri, born in 1867.

Marguerite, born in 1869.

Jean-Pierre-Clémence-Marie, born in 1874.

X.

THE COMTE DE PARIS.

---

*His Childhood.—His Escape From the Revolution.—His
Youth and Travels.—Soldier, Author, and Linguist.*

HE ENTERS THE U. S. ARMY.

---

*His Sudden Departure.—His Marriage.—His Conspiracies
Against the French Republic.—His Banishment.*

At the time of the revolution, of February,
1848, the Comte de Paris was barely ten years
old. His childhood was spent abroad, in Germany, England, Spain and America, but the
remembrance of the 24th of February has
never, he says, been effaced from his memory.

On the morning of the 22d, they came to inform the Comte de Paris that the masters who
ought to have given him his lessons could not
come. Not being old enough to understand
exactly all that was taking place, he was nevertheless able to take note of the preoccupations of his mother and of the other persons
who were about.

The 24th, when the Duchess of Orleans came to kiss her son, she said to him, "My dear child, you must know that grave events are taking place ; you cannot understand them ; but pray to God and he will, perhaps, turn aside the great misfortunes with which France is threatened."

In the morning Mr. Adolphe Regnier, the young prince's tutor, since a member of the Institute, gave him, notwithstanding, his lessons as usual, but they had soon to leave the room which looked out on the Rue de Rivoli ; they expected any moment a fight ; the prince went to the apartments looking on to the garden.

As he was playing under the eyes of his tutor the door opened suddenly and the Duchess of Orleans entered, saying to Mr. Regnier, "It is not a riot, it is a revolution!" The child had too often heard the previous revolutions talked about, not to understand already the significance of the word.

The Duchess of Orleans, seeing the turn that events were taking, went in to the queen ; she began to feel very uneasy for her son, and resolved not to be separated from him, wished to keep him near her. Mr. Regnier had followed her ; the child and his tutor were put in the bedroom which separated Louis-Philippe's cabinet from that of the queen, Marie-Amélie. There, with a certain degree of sang-froid, the tutor, not to allow his pupil to give way to vague uneasiness, tried to continue the lesson already commenced.

The prince was then translating the *Epitome Historiæ Sacræ,* of Lhomond ; he has never forgotten that they had reached that portion of the history of the Maccabees where the young heroes perished in a caldron of boiling oil. The image of this caldron was for a long time mixed up in his imagination with the real scenes in which he took a part.

Soon they came to inform the king that the troops assembled on the Place du Carrousel wished to see him. Louis-Philippe went out, and the child went to the window to see his grandfather pass them in review. Emotion had also taken possession of him, and he was visibly impressed by the cries of "Long live the king!" which were still heard on all sides. He was also much struck at hearing the name of Marshal Bugeaud frequently pronounced.

Time passes on ; the king was still in the courtyard ; then all at once the door of the cabinet opens suddenly, and Louis Philippe, standing erect in the doorway, says, with a firm, serious voice, "I am going to abdicate."

This word pierced the Comte de Paris' mind like a flash of lightning, and with an energy beyond his years, he ran to his tutor, saying, "No, it is impossible." He was naturally unable to take into account the terrible responsibilities which weigh upon modern royalty ; but he understood at once that if his grandfather abdicated they would put him in his place on a gilded throne, he would have to figure in all the official ceremonies, the eyes of all would be turned upon him ; this idea was insupportable to him.

Nevertheless the royal chamber became deserted.   Here and there, on the Place du Carousel, guns were fired.   The young prince is no longer allowed to look out of the window. The Duchess of Orleans goes to her apartments ; she finds in the Gallery de la Paix a few members of the household who join her.

She descends to the pavilion de Marsan, where a few political men are assembled, amongst others Mr. Dupin and Admiral Baudin, who urge her to go to the Chamber of Deputies.   She remains but a moment, and leaves by the Court du Carousel.

The court is empty ; one hears every now and then a gun fired, as if at random, at the Tuilleries ; they pass on under the pavilion de l' Horloge, and thus abandon the Palace of the Tuilleries.

While crossing its beautiful garden the count hears it said that they will find carriages on the Place de la Concorde, and that they will take them and go for a drive around Paris, and thus save the situation.   This advice had been given by some political men who had penetrated into the garden. At the railings of the drawbridge they stop; the carriages are not there, and a compact and swaying mob invades the space occupied by a battery of artillery, whose movements it paralyzes.

The commandant places himself at the disposal of the duchess. Mr. Adolphe Regnier recognizes in the officer one of his intimate friends, and names him to his pupil. It was Tiby, chief of squadron, who, in later years, as a retired colonel, was killed in the Rue de la Paix by the balls of the Commune, on the day of the pacific manifestation.

At length the Duchess of Orleans is informed that the Duke of Nemours will accompany her and her sons to the Chamber of Deputies. He arrives at the same time, and the group, which he has joined at the garden gate, wends its way through the crowd and reaches the Palais-Bourbon.

The Comte de Paris had been present for the first time, a few days previously, at the opening of the Chambers. The aspect of the assembly was therefore not new to him. The deputies were in session, and the hall in which their deliberations had been held had not yet been invaded. The Duchess of Orleans and her sons entered and took their places in that part of the hall reserved for deputies.

At the first the Comte de Paris was unable to clearly understand what was going on. He was seated near his mother, at the foot of the bureau on the left. After having heard from that position the first speakers who succeeded each other at the tribune, the duchess had to move up to one of the highest seats in the centre. Soon the count heard some one say to his mother : "It is Mr. *Marie* who is speaking." This name, which seemed to him to be a woman's, struck him, and he will never forget it.

He looks about him and smiles at Mr. de Rémusat, seated at his side, then, a few moments after, he sees someone coming towards them, whose shock of hair has ever remained in his young memory as one of the most remarkable things which he saw at this sitting; it was Mr. Crémieux, a future member of the National Defense in 1870-71, who wrote a few words on a sheet of paper and handed it to the duchess, saying : "Here are the words which I advise you to address to the Chamber."

The Comte de Paris no longer paid any attention to what was said at the tribune, he was too much occupied with what was going on around him. His mother, however, was surrounded by many of the deputies, some advising her to speak, and others, on the contrary to wait.

It was then that the boy heard distinctly the

violent blows which shook the doors of the
hall. The rioters howl, the doors burst open,
the crowd rushes into the hall, the tumult is
terrible. The duchess and her sons are in
danger. Mr. de Rémusat places himself in
front of the Comte de Paris to shield his body.
As the danger is imminent, they decide the
duchess to leave the Chamber ; she fears for
the life of her children and consents to go out
with them by one of the relief passages. But
in this confusion, the Comte de Paris and the
Duke de Chartres are pushed or rather dragged
by the crowd, some threatening, some en-
deavouring to protect them. They stop at last
at a distant room of the president's, situated
on the ground floor, where the invaders have
not penetrated. There they look to see that
none are missing ; the duchess of Orleans finds
only her eldest son. Mr. Regnier, in the con-
fused and hurried exit, had been for a moment
separated from him, but was enabled almost
immediately to join him again and brought
him to his mother.

The Duke de Chartres had also been borne
away in another direction ; and as the duchess,
anxious, wished to turn back, they assure her
that the young prince is safe. The duke had been,
in effect knocked down by the crowd ; but Mr.
Lipman, brother of one of the sergeants of the
Chamber, picked him up and carried him away
to the apartment which his brother occupied

in the dependencies of the palace and where already a few moments previously, he had offered shelter to Mr. Regnier and his ycungest son.

But they are still too near; the tide advances, they are again obliged to move; they descend into the garden and go out by the Rue de Lille. There they find a cab; the Duchess of Orleans gets in with her sons; two national guards, Messrs. L. Martinet and David, follow them and offer to protect her; the vehicle takes the direction of the Hotel des Invalides, where the fugitives take shelter in a room, in which they find Marshal Molitor, and then they part for their long exile.

Brought up in the little town of Eisenach—where his mother had taken up her residence—and after completing his literary studies, the count set himself seriously to the study of the applied sciences.

Numerous excursions in Europe made him familiar with the ideas and languages of several foreign countries, specially of England, where his paternal relatives now resided.

After making, with his brother, a long voyage in the East, the comte wrote a relation of his adventures, which was published under the title "*Damascus and Lebanon*" (London, 1861.)

The Comte de Paris had been residing some time in England when the War of Secession

broke out in the United States. He embarked
with his brother, the Duke de Chartres, for
the New World, and, as he wished to draw
attention to himself, he entered the Federal
army as a volunteer. Both were at once
nominated staff-captains (29th September,
1861), and were attached as aides-de-camp to
McClellan, then at the head of the army of
the Potomac; made under his orders a fruit-
less campaign against Richmond, assisted at
the siege of York-Town, at the battles of
Williamsburg, Fair-Oaks, Gaine's Mill, at the
retreat of the Federal army on the James
River. Then, for reasons variously appre-
ciated, they both left the Federal army and
returned to Europe in 1863.

Married the 30th of May, 1864, to Princesse
Marie-Isabella, daughter of his uncle, the
Duke de Montpensier, the Comte de Paris has
two sons and four daughters.* The eldest,
son and heir,

PRINCE LOUIS-PHILIPPE-ROBERT D'ORLÉANS,

Born at York House, near Twickenham, the
6th February, 1869, is the same who, on attain-
ing his majority, was recently condemned to
two years' imprisonment for infringing the

---

* Marie-Amélie-Hélène, born in 1865, married in 1886 to
Charles, Crown Prince, and to-day King of Portugal,
  Héléne-Louise-Henriette, born in 1871,
  Marie-Isabelle, born in 1878,
  Louise-Françoise, born in 1882, and
  Ferdinand-François, born in 1884.

laws of exile, his sentence being, however, re-
mitted by President Carnot two months afterwards.

When war was declared against Prussia the
Comte de Paris, as well as the other princes
of his family, asked permission to enter the
French army in any grade whatsoever. Their
application was rejected, the 11th August, by
the legislative body.

Returning to France after the abrogation of
the laws of exile, the Comte de Paris held
himself at first aloof from all politics, but, unfortunately for himself, he did not continue in
this wise course.

His father, the Duke d'Orléans, had written
in his will : " Whether the Comte de Paris be
" king or remain an unknown and obscure
" defender of a cause to which we all belong,
" he must above all be a man of his times and
" of the nation, the impassioned and exclusive
" servitor of France and of the Revolution."

Forgetful of the paternal wishes, the Comte
de Paris, following up a series of preparatory
negociations which lasted some months, at a
time when the monarchical party, after having
overthrown Thiers, seemed completely master
of the situation, and had inaugurated against
the Republic and the Republicans the Government of Combat, the Comte de Paris went to
Frohsdorf the 5th August, 1873, to make his
submission, saying to the Count of Chambord,

who, as is well known, had no offspring : " I
" come to pay you a visit which has been for
" a long time on my mind. I salute in you, in
" the name of all the members of my family
" and in my own name, not only the chief of
" our house, but also the only representative
" of monarchical principles in France."

By this step the Comte de Paris, who had
become the presumptive heir of the monarchy
of divine right, aimed a blow at the Orleanist
party, which considered him its chief. The
Republic has made the mistake of showing
itself too generous to him and to his family.
Forty millions, received immediately after the
Franco-Prussian War, and high grades in the
army could not satisfy their inordinate ambition. They began to conspire. Then the
Republic finished where it should have
begun. In '83 it voted the laws of exile
against all the heirs of the families who
had reigned in France, and took from
them their grades in the army, to which they
had no right whatsoever.

Physically, the Comte de Paris is powerful
and quite tall, very blond and becoming now
gray ; he has the essentially German type.

Morally, he is an intelligent man. Besides
his history of the War of Secession, he has
published a certain number of volumes which
have met with fair success.

XI.

FRENCH OPINION OF THE PRINCES.

In France the Princes of Orleans are neither beloved nor hated. Apart from any personal esteem which they may inspire, indifference is the only sentiment which they call forth.

Politically speaking, love of money has killed them. After the Franco-German War, when France, still bleeding, mutilated and crushed, was almost too weak to raise herself from beneath the terribly heavy burden of the fifteen billions imposed upon her by her disasters, the princes, with a heartless indifference to her sufferings, found means through the then existing reactionary government to wrest from the National Treasury forty millions, which they unhesitatingly appropriated. To say the least, the moment was ill chosen, and everyone must feel that it would have been an act of generous patriotism on their part had they abandoned that sum for the benefit of their unhappy country. But they thought otherwise. France, therefore, paid them, but at the same time repudiated them, and she is to day no more royalist than Bonapartist. Nothing remains of its former monarchical constitution.

For the last twenty years that she governs herself, tranquilly, without evil passions, without injurious provocations, without any kind of fanaticism, she shows to the world that she is perfectly capable of directing her course, without tutors, without protectors, without the aid of any authority whatsoever. She has resolved to remain irrevocably attached to democratic principles and to tolerate no longer any masters, should they declare themselves sent by God or pretend to be the elect of the people ; and, if peradventure the noble count should ever manifest the pretension to command France under the title of Philippe VII., she would undoubtedly answer him with those so well deserved words which Elizabeth sent to his Homonyme, Philippe II : "*Ad græcas, bone rex, fiant mandata calendas.* * *"

[THE END.]

GENEALOGICAL TABLE OF THE BOURBONS FROM HENRI IV.

HENRI IV + 1610.

Branche aînée –

Branche cadette.

Louis XIII, + 1643.

Gaston d'Orléans. + 1660.

Philippe, duc d'Orléans, + 1701. (Root of the 2nd house of Orleans.)

Philippe II. Regent, + 1723.

Louis, + 1752.

Louis-Philippe, + 1785.

Louis-Philippe-Joseph, (Egalité) + 1793.

Louis-Philippe I. (King) + 1850.

{ Dukes d'Orleans. (Title of the eldest son or principal heir of the house.) }

Louis XIV, + 1715.

Louis, dauphin, + 1711.

Louis, Duke de Bourgogne, + 1712.

Louis XV, + 1774.

Louis, dauphin, + 1765.

Louis XVI, + 1793.

Louis XVIII, + 1824.

Charles X, + 1836.

Louis, dauphin, (Louis XVII) + 1795.

Duke d'Angoulême, + 1840.

Duke de Berry + 1820.

Marie-Thérèse Duchess d'Angoulême + 1851.

Henri, Duke de Bordeaux. (Comte de Chambord.) Born 1820, + 1883.

Louise-Marie-Thérèse Born 1849.

Ferdinand-Philippe, Duke d' Orléans. + 1842.

Philippe, Comte de Paris. Born 1838.

Duke de Chartres. Born 1840.

Prince Louis-Philippe-Robert d'Orléans. Born 1869.

Louis-Marie, Queen of Belgium + 1850.

Duke de Nemours, born 1814.

Marie-Christine, Duchess of Würtemburg 1813.

Marie-Clémentine, born 1817.

Prince de Joinville   – 1818.

Duke d'Aumale   –   1822.

Duke de Montpensier   –   1824.

Marie-Isabelle-Amélie   –

Isabelle-Louise-Amélie, born 1871.

Marie-Amélie   –

Louis-Amédée   –   1845.

Ferdinand-Napoléon   –   1884.

www.ingramcontent.com/pod-product-compliance
Lightning Source LLC
Chambersburg PA
CBHW031322280626
47169CB00019B/2612